For Daisy
and Rose Riordan

Copyright © 1992 by Ruth Brown
All rights reserved.
CIP Data is available.
First published in the United States 1993 by
Dutton Children's Books,
a division of Penguin Books USA Inc.
375 Hudson Street, New York, New York 10014
Originally published in Great Britain 1992
by Andersen Press Ltd.
Printed in Italy
Typography by Adrian Leichter
First American Edition
1 3 5 7 9 10 8 6 4 2
ISBN 0-525-45091-2

ONE STORMY NIGHT

BY **Ruth Brown**

Dutton Children's Books   New York

One stormy night, the wind was howling.

The iron gate creaked

and the black cat hissed.

Inside, the firelight flickered

and, roused from sleep,
the old dog barked.

The great oak door of the barn flew open.

The gray mare stared

and a white owl screeched.

Then, just before dawn, the wind fell silent.
The sky was clear and a bright star shone.

For many, a new day was beginning.

But others slept on

in the morning sun.